The Arrowhead Detectives

in The

Mystery

of the

Disappearing Baby

JACK WHITE

ISBN 979-8-88751-843-5 (paperback)
ISBN 979-8-88751-844-2 (digital)

Christian Faith Publishing
832 Park Avenue
Meadville, PA 16335
www.christianfaithpublishing.com

Printed in the United States of America

To my beloved wife, Ann. Her encouragement and suggestions helped me complete this writing.

I want the world to know that I'm truly blessed to have such a wife who is this fantastic and whom we love and cherish very much.

To my daughter and son, whom I love and whom I named my two leading characters after, Penny and Larry. My true and deepest love to my family.

The Mystery of the
Disappearing Baby

Contents

Author's Note

The names of places and characters are fictional. Should they match the names of people and places elsewhere, it *is* coincidental.

Sheriff Ralph Rivers and his wife, Denise, are the parents of Larry and Penny, two members of the Arrowhead Detective Team.

Isaac and Elizabeth (Beth) Lightner are the parents of Ted, Faith, and Cherry, three members of the Arrowhead Detective Team. Isaac is a successful real estate agent.

Larry and Ted are now twenty-one and just a few months out of military service with honorable discharges. They entered the service at age eighteen and did three years in the Pacific Northwest.

Their military service was with the military police.

Penny's, Faith's, and Cherry's ages range from eighteen to twenty.

The Arrowhead Mystery Detectives and Arrowhead County is a work of fiction and the stories pertaining to it that I have written are fictitious as well. These are meant for reading enjoyment only.

I would also like to give my deep-hearted thank you to *all* law enforcement agencies: county, state, and federal officials. My family and I give all of you our deep-hearted thank you and respect for your protection in our society (1 Timothy 2:2–3).

Thank you.

Jack

The Arrowhead Detectives

They came from rural America, dedicated to their God, dedicated to their country, dedicated to the preservation of freedom and the pursuit of happiness.

Nothing is too great a task for them that they would risk and, if need be, give their very lives to save life and limb of those that seek their help. When they take a case, they take it to solve it and keep at it until they are finished, and to know that they have done it to the best of their ability.

Larry Rivers is their captain. At times, he has to make decisions that affect them all one way or another. His build is tall and muscular with deep brown hair and a deep complexion.

Ted Lightner is the team's electronic and photography expert. His knowledge of this special work is invaluable because it is of immense importance to the others as they work to help others that are in need of their help. Ted's build is tall and muscular with black hair and a deep complexion.

Penny Rivers is the cocaptain. As do the others, she studies the challenges from all sides and uses caution to stop those that wish to do harm. She has long blonde hair and a light, pretty complexion with a very pretty smile.

Faith Lightner does research for the team that helps in all their cases that they accept so that they can obtain the truth and uphold justice. She has short brown hair with a fair complexion and a pretty smile.

Cherry Lightner keeps records of all their cases should they need them for future reference to a previous case. Like her colleagues, she stands ready to defend her country and community from those that seek to do injustice and inflict harm. She has short, dark brunette hair with a light complexion and a pretty smile.

Putting together their every effort, they form one of America's best detective teams. Follow Larry, Ted, Penny, Faith, and Cherry as they work with Sheriff Ralph Rivers of Arrowhead County. Located in the foothills of the Great Smoky Mountains of Western North Carolina, the young team, known as the Arrowhead Detectives, match wits with the best of the criminals around. But try as they might, the criminals cannot outwit Larry's superb mind and keen eye, and those of his four detective colleagues.

You'll be amazed at what happens next. They'll lead you into spine-tingling adventures that will keep you on the edge of your chair.

You're invited to come along on each adventure to see how everything comes out and to follow them as they dare to travel the danger-filled roads to excitement, knowing that their Lord is keeping them safe through it all.

One

A Baby Is Left

The fire crackled and gave a great warmth into the living room.

"This may be an August night," blond-haired, light-complected Mrs. Rivers said, moving toward the fireplace. "But it sure feels like winter to me."

"It is rather cool," Larry Rivers said, putting another split log on the fire.

The front door opened and in walked a black-haired, dark-complected, uniformed man, his sheriff's badge glistening in the firelight.

"Hello, Daddy," Penny Rivers said cheerfully.

"Hello, all," the sheriff said. "That fire feels good. If I didn't know better, I'd say this was a winter night instead of an August night. It really is cool outside."

He moved up to the fireplace as Larry said, "That is why I built the fire."

"It sure feels good," the sheriff repeated slowly. His smile turned into a frown as he stared into the dancing flames. Mrs. Rivers knew that something was not right.

"What's wrong?" she asked tenderly.

"There was a kidnapping today," he replied.

"Oh no!" Penny exclaimed softly.

"It was a two-month-old baby," Sheriff Rivers explained. "Kidnapping an older person is bad enough but kidnapping a two-month-old baby just tears me up."

He turned toward the others as Larry asked, "Are there any leads yet?"

"It was taken from the orphanage in White Pine. About ten this morning was when the baby was discovered missing," the sheriff explained.

"How could anyone kidnap a helpless baby?" Mrs. Rivers wondered aloud. "They ought to be…" She suddenly stopped. With a puzzled look, she turned toward the kitchen door.

"What's wrong?" the sheriff inquired.

"I thought I heard a baby crying at the back door," she said. "I don't hear it now."

They listened for a few more seconds, but the only sound they heard was the rustling of the cold wind through the trees.

"I believe that you are so upset about the kidnapping that you are hearing babies from out of nowhere," the sheriff said with a chuckle. "Let's eat supper, and I believe we'll all feel better."

"Perhaps you are right," she agreed. "You know how I am when it comes to children and their welfare. I fall apart if anything happens to them."

They went into the kitchen and went about putting supper on the table. Just as they were sitting down, they heard glass break outside their back door.

"Now I know I heard that!" Mrs. Rivers exclaimed, going to the back door with the others following. She opened the back door, and on the porch, they saw a small baby in a carrying cradle wrapped in some blankets. Lying beside the cradle was a broken baby bottle.

"To the heavens above!" Mrs. Rivers exclaimed.

She picked the cradle up and took it into the kitchen. Larry got a broom and cleaned the broken glass up and joined the others at the table.

"It can't be more than a few months old," Penny observed.

"It's a wonder that it did not freeze to death in this weather," Mrs. Rivers remarked, feeling the baby's cheeks. "His face is cold, but the rest of him is warm."

The sheriff went to the phone and dialed a number. Seconds later, he said, "This is Sheriff Rivers…" He paused a few minutes and then replied, "Thank you very much." He hung up the phone and turned toward the others. "The kidnappers were arrested in a restaurant over toward Passville when they attempted a robbery at two this afternoon."

"But who left this baby…," Penny started but was interrupted by the telephone. The sheriff answered it.

As he listened, his eyes got big as quarters. He hung up the phone and looked at the clock, which had six thirty. He looked at his family and replied, "That was the state patrol, and they said the kidnappers escaped at about 5:00 p.m. and were last seen coming this way. They also had the baby with them. They somehow managed to kidnap the baby again from the welfare service this time."

His words were no sooner spoken when a dull thud came from the front door. Larry, being the first one there, opened the door and found a flaming arrow stuck in the door. He pulled it out and extinguished the fire. The back door suddenly slammed shut, and they raced back into the kitchen and saw that the baby was gone. A note lay in its place. The sheriff read its contents aloud.

"Don't try to follow or it's death you'll meet!"

"Find it here and you'll find it sweet."

"What does that mean?" Mrs. Rivers asked.

Before anyone could answer, the phone rang, and Larry answered.

"Help me!" a woman's voice shouted into the phone. Before Larry could reply, a loud horrid scream came over the wire, and then the phone went dead!

Two

A Visit to Sheriff Rivers

"Lunch was delicious, Mrs. Rivers," Ted Lightner responded. "Thanks for the invitation."

"You're quite welcome," Mrs. Rivers said with a warm smile. "And thanks for helping around the house."

Ted, his two sisters, Faith and Cherry, and their mom and dad, Elizabeth and Isaac, are very good friends of the Rivers family. Ted had come over to help Larry work on his model railroad, and the girls were working on some curtains that were to be hung up in the living room and kitchen.

Ted looked at Larry. "You say you've no other clues as to who may have taken the baby?"

"Not a sign," Larry answered. Larry and Penny had related the events of the night before to the others.

"Only that mysterious note that we found on the kitchen table," Penny said.

"The note is interesting," Larry commented. "I cannot find any meaning in its words, and I studied it over until two this morning. I'm going to ask Dad if he can get us information as to who put that note on our table. Maybe the lab has come up with something."

"I hope Daddy has some good news," Penny replied. "This whole thing bothers me."

Larry looked at his sister. "I'm not exactly overjoyed by this myself," he sighed.

"I hope the baby is alright," Faith stated in a worried tone.

"That is unanimous," Ted replied.

"Let's go see what Dad's office has," Larry said.

*****   *****   *****

"The sheriff says he'll see you," the secretary said, pointing to a door marked "SHERIFF."

They filed into the office and sat down on the sofa against the far wall. Sheriff Rivers looked at his visitors. He smiled as he asked, "And what can I do for you?"

"Has the lab found any prints on that note that was left on our kitchen table?" Larry asked.

"Yes, a couple," the sheriff explained. "After a thorough search of our files, we find that the prints belong to a man who was released from prison. He was serving time for bank robbery, drug smuggling, kidnapping, and interstate flight to avoid prosecution. His name is Joe Chambers."

"Chambers!" Ted exclaimed, taking a new interest.

"You know him?" the sheriff asked.

"Dad said something the other day about a Joe Chambers buying the old Bruntner place," Ted explained, referring to his dad's real estate business. "Dad said that Chambers gave three times what Bruntner was asking. Bruntner was asking $50,000, and Chambers gave $150,000 cash for the old house and the twelve acres that go with it. Dad said that Chambers gave the money very gladly and with great interest."

"He gave cash?" the sheriff asked, showing interest.

"The plot thickens," Larry said.

"But why did he put the note on our table?" Penny asked.

"He didn't," the sheriff answered.

Larry and the others looked at the sheriff. "He didn't?" Larry and Penny asked in unison.

"His alibi was proven for last night," Sheriff Rivers said. "We were looking for him when an individual verified that he was with him. Along with him, a gas station attendant also said that he was with them when they stopped for gas. We believe that an accomplice put the note on our table, but we don't know who."

"We might be able to find a clue at the old house," Ted said.

"I was going to ask you if there was any way that we could get into the old house without Chambers knowing it," Larry said.

"I'm one step ahead of you," the sheriff replied. "Chambers knows that patrols would be coming by the old house to check on him. He knows I don't trust him."

"How does that get us into the old house?" Larry asked.

"The first patrol to go out there," the sheriff replied, "is you."

Larry was surprised and after a few minutes his response was, "Me, huh?"

"Yes, you." Sheriff Rivers looked at his watch. "It is now 1:00 p.m. Your shift starts at three.

Larry looked at the wall clock behind his dad's desk and said, "This ought to be good!"

Three

Larry's Hunch

Larry looked at himself in the hall mirror. "Dad really surprised me with this one," he said, combing his hair. He also adjusted his uniform tie.

"He surprised us all," Penny replied. "When are you going to the old house?"

"At three thirty," Larry answered, looking at his watch. "That's the first part of my patrol."

As he finished, the grandfather clock in the living room struck the half hour, indicating 2:30 p.m.

*****   *****   *****

Even though the sun was shining brightly through the trees, the old house still loomed with an uninviting, cold atmosphere as Larry stopped in front of the worn, colonial-style doors that were badly in need of some fresh paint as was the rest of the house. Larry slid from behind the wheel of his two-tone blue patrol truck and walked to the front of and studied the old house. He took a deep breath and approached the two big front doors. He adjusted his holster and rang the doorbell. It was a lonely echo Larry heard as the bell rang through the house. After what seemed like forever and a day, the doors opened and a big man with dark skin and a mean scowl looked down at Larry. Seeing his uniform, he growled, "You the patrolman that's supposed to come around?"

"Y-yes," Larry stammered, forcing the words from his throat, trying to show courage.

His burly host threw open the door. "Come in. Can't stand here all day."

Larry walked in and the man slammed the door shut. Larry was escorted into the living room. He noticed that most of the furniture had white covers over them. On one table in the corner by the fireplace were some photo albums. *I must look through them the first chance I get*, he thought to himself.

"What's your name?" Larry's host bellowed out.

"Larry Rivers," he replied.

"Rivers?" the man mused, his voice calmer. "Are you any kin to Sheriff Rivers?"

"Yes, he's my dad," Larry said.

"Your dad's a good man," the husky man replied. "You ought to make a good patrolman." His voice became more tender. "I need you."

For the first time, Larry noticed the faraway look in the man's eyes. They began to moisten as he looked at Larry. "I need your help," he pleaded in a meek voice and he was almost on the brink of tears.

*****   *****   *****

Meanwhile, Ted was checking a lead Larry had told him.

"Larry said that the second line of the note read, 'Find it here and you'll find it sweet,'" Ted explained.

"What have you two come up with?" Faith asked.

"There's a lot of interest in the old Bruntner place," Ted explained. "While Larry was getting his uniform, he came up with the idea that maybe there's something hidden at the old house that would have to do with being sweet. I'm going to check it out. Even though I have a walkie-talkie, I need you, girls, here to call in backup units in case I need them, and I can't."

"Ted Lightner!" Cherry put in. "It's too dangerous!"

Ted looked at his youngest sister. "It's also too dangerous for the baby, but someone has got to go get him."

"Then I'm going with you!" she declared as she left the house in a very determined manner and firmly sat down in Ted's truck.

"That's our little sister," Ted replied with a smile. He looked at Faith and Penny and handed them a walkie-talkie. "I'll call in every half-hour."

"You be careful," Faith said.

"Let us know how Larry is," Penny requested.

"I sure will," Ted agreed. He kissed the girls on the forehead goodbye and walked out to his four-wheel truck.

***** ***** *****

The time was 4:00 p.m. as Ted looked at his watch. He had parked his truck on a hill overlooking the old house.

"We walk from here," Ted instructed.

They both walked down the old path that hadn't been used in years. The brush around them was so thick they could not see a thing through the trees and bushes. Both agreed the brush could no doubt stop a tank. They worked their way to the back of the old house and saw several buildings. One in particular caught Ted's eye. He noticed something odd but could not quite put his finger on it. He was about to say something to Cherry when there came a dull thud, and he blacked out.

Four

No Doors or Windows

Slowly, Ted opened his eyes, and it took a few minutes to get his bearings. All he could see was darkness. He suddenly felt around him. He could not find his flashlight nor could he find his walkie-talkie. He sat back and gave a small sigh. A minute or two later, he heard moans.

"Cherry!" he suddenly thought. In a quiet tone, he inquired into the darkness, "Sis?"

"What hit me?" she groaned, rubbing her head.

"I don't know," Ted replied as he helped his sister sit up. "I sure would like to get hold of it, or him."

They both sat there a minute or two as Cherry looked around her. It was hard to see anything. She slowly moved her hand around on the floor and wall. All she could feel was wood.

"Where are we?" she asked.

"I'd say somewhere in the old house, if not on the estate grounds," Ted answered. "They've taken my flashlight and walkie-talkie as well."

"Great!" Cherry responded. "I can't even see you."

"I can fix that," Ted assured her.

"What do you mean?" his sister asked.

Ted held a lighter and lit it to throw light into the room. He could see his sister's astonished face.

"A good detective always comes well prepared for just such an emergency as this," he said with a grin.

Ted helped his sister to her feet as she said, "I should have known you would come up with something." She looked at Ted and continued. "Let's look around and see if we cannot find our way out of here."

"Why didn't I think of that?" Ted wondered aloud as he looked around their wooden cell.

All they could see were wood boards that made the cell. Ted examined each board on the wall. All he found was wood and nails. Cherry was tapping lightly at some boards at the other end. They were tightly secured. Ted tapped again on some boards at eye level but found them well in place. Close examination of the floor was fruitless. Ted guessed the size of their cell to be about twelve feet long by eight feet wide by ten feet high.

"If we can find no doors, then how did we get in here?" Cherry puzzled. "It's as if there are no doors or windows."

"There has to be!" Ted declared. "How else were we put in here?"

Both sat down in silence. Ted glanced at his watch. "The time is 9:30 p.m. Penny and Faith are no doubt wondering about us. It has been over five hours."

Silence unfolded in the room again. Both sat waiting and wondering who had put them in here and why. Ted looked around him again. There was something about the room that kept nagging at him, but he could not quite grasp hold of it. Cherry looked at the ceiling and then motioned for Ted to look up. Slowly turning his head upward, he saw a small light coming through the boards. He slowly sat up, and as he did so, the light disappeared.

Ted started to scale the wall, getting a finger hold where he could. About four feet up, his fingers slipped, and he fell to the floor. He slowly sat up as his youngest sister helped him. Ted sat there studying the ceiling. Cherry relit the lighter that had fallen from Ted's shirt pocket during the fall. Suddenly, Ted sat straight up. He put his hand over the flame and looked at the ceiling.

"What is it?" Cherry asked.

As he moved his hand, they both saw the flame. But, when Ted covered the light again, it vanished. Looking at each other, they whispered together, "A mirror!"

Ted stood to his feet and took Cherry by the hand as they walked to one end of the room. Ted took his pocketknife and threw it upward at the mirrored ceiling. It struck but did not break the mirror. Ted picked up his knife and tried it again with a harder throw.

This time, the mirror shattered and fell to the floor. Beyond the opening, the night sky twinkled with brightly shining stars. But before either one could move, an ear-piercing alarm sounded, breaking the quiet stillness of the night.

Five

Eleventh Hour Scream

"I'm not leaving you here by yourself!" Cherry proclaimed.

"This is no time to argue!" Ted yelled above the sound of the alarm as he interlocked his fingers. "Put your foot in my hands, and I'll boost you up."

Within seconds, Cherry was standing at the edge of their prison looking down at her brother. "I'll find a rope and throw it down to you!"

Before Ted could respond, she was out of sight. Ted studied the top for a second or two, and he backed up to the other end.

*****   *****   *****

Cherry, meanwhile, had found some bailing twine in a nearby shed, and she rushed back to where Ted was at. She got the rope ready to drop to Ted when strong arms pulled her into the shadows. She froze solid until she heard a familiar voice whisper, "It's only me, Sis."

Ted released his grasp and Cherry looked around at her brother. Her voice was stern but was also full of relief. "You scared five years of life out of me. How did you get out of there?"

"I flew," he said taking her by the hand and leading her toward the house. At the front door, Ted slowly opened it, and they went in. They found themselves in what was the living room at one time.

"Larry said that he would meet us here," Ted explained. "After you went to get the twine, I took a running leap across our prison and was able to scale up the wall. After I was outside, I found myself in the midst of oncoming footsteps, and I hid in the bushes. I saw two big men who went down the path. A few minutes later, Larry approached the wooden hole we were in, and I came out of my hiding place and explained the entire story to him. He asked me to wait here with you, and he would join us here."

"Where did he go?" Cherry asked.

"To call the sheriff," came a voice from across the room.

Ted and Cherry looked toward the door that led to the back of the house, and they saw Larry standing there. "I was coming down the road and when I heard the alarm and then I called Dad and reported what had happened," he continued. "I also asked him to call Penny and Faith and tell them you two are all right. Dad said he would go by and get them and bring them out here with him. Once they are all here, I'll fill you in on what I have found. With what we have, it should make for quite an interesting case."

While they waited, Ted and Cherry looked through the mountain of old albums that Larry had seen earlier. The pictures were old and showed various buildings and other scenes around the old estate. There was one picture that showed the foundation of an old building. "Look familiar?" Ted questioned handing the picture to Cherry.

"Yes!" she said without hesitation. "I have no desire to see that old prison again." Cherry looked at her watch and continued. "It's 11:00 p.m. Shouldn't the others be here by now?"

"They should've been," Larry said. "It's been over two hours since I called."

"What say one of us go and see what has happened," Ted suggested.

There was a sharp knock at the door, and everyone turned and looked at it. Finally, Larry approached the door slowly. The knocking continued until he reached the door. He swung it open to find his beaten, soaking wet sister standing there, leaning against the door frame.

"Sis!" he exclaimed as he helped her inside.

Setting her down in a chair, Larry looked at Cherry. "Please go out to my patrol truck and bring me the first-aid kit. It's behind the seat."

With his handkerchief, Larry wiped her forehead and face gently. Within a few minutes, Cherry returned with the first-aid kit and Larry finished cleaning Penny's cut and put a bandage on the nasty bruise above her left eye. "That will do until she can get better medical attention," Larry said.

"I feel like a train has hit me," Penny said, slowly sitting up.

"I would say from the size of that cut," Ted observed. "You're going to have a headache for a while."

"Don't remind me," Penny said, holding her head.

"How did this happen?" Larry asked.

"We were on our way out here when someone forced us off the road," Penny explained. I don't know who, and I don't know why. All I know is that it happened. We were thrown from Daddy's patrol car, and Daddy and Faith are still unconscious or were when I left the car."

Before anyone could speak, there came a rock in through the window, sending glass everywhere. Ted gently picked it up and removed the note that was tied to it. He gave the note to Larry as he laid the rock down. Larry opened the note and read its contents as they gathered around him. "Either leave or face the consequences." Below this was written another message: "They make a sound like a rattle, you better hope you never engage them in battle."

Everyone looked at one another. "What does it mean?" Penny asked. Before anyone could say anything, there came an ear-shattering scream from outside.

Six

Wounded Visitor

"That's the same scream I heard at home over the telephone!" Larry exclaimed when the screaming had stopped.

"Let's go see who it is," Penny put in.

Everyone looked at her as Larry asked, "Are you sure that you can see straight with that nasty cut?"

"I made here from across Hazardous Creek," she said.

Ted gave a low whistle. Everyone was familiar with Hazardous Creek. Even when the creek was low, it was still a tough crossing because of the steep slope and slippery rocks that dotted the creek.

"I came that way," Penny explained. "Because it's also a shortcut over to here."

"Let's go, then," Larry instructed. Looking at his sister, he stated, "Stay close and don't wander off."

They went out the door and looked around the old yard that was overgrown with weeds and thorns that were so thick, the growth would stump a brush-hog. Ted flashed his light toward the growth of oak trees. He pointed in that direction, and everyone saw a figure stretched out behind a tree, all they could see were the feet. Slowly, they walked that way, and Larry looked at her face. A blonde-haired woman was unconscious, her face was muddy, and some blood was on her blouse at the right shoulder. Knowing something about extensive first-aid, Larry examined the wound. He said to the others, "It went through, she has lost a lot of blood, and we have to get her to a doctor."

Larry picked her up and carried her to the back of his truck. Then the girls made the wounded woman as comfortable as possible.

"Let's get Faith and Daddy," Larry said, climbing in behind the wheel.

"I'll meet you there," Ted replied, going to his truck.

***** ***** *****

"Let's have a look at that nasty cut," the doctor said, taking the bandage off Penny's forehead.

Larry and the others were in the emergency room of Lakeville hospital. The doctor slowly removed the bandage from Penny's forehead as Larry asked, "What about Dad and Faith?"

"They will be fine," the doctor assured them. "Like Penny, they will have a headache for a while."

"How is the woman we found?" Cherry asked.

"The surgery went fine," the doctor explained. "After lots of rest and some good hot meals, she'll be fine, also."

Dressing Penny's cut, he asked, "What was she doing up there?"

"We're not exactly sure," Larry answered vaguely. "We do know that she wasn't up there for a midnight stroll." After a minute, Larry continued. "We'd like to see Dad and Faith."

"Sure," the doctor agreed. "They've been asking to see you as well. They're in treatment room 2."

After the doctor had finished dressing Penny's cut, the three walked back to treatment room 2 and met a nurse coming out. She held the door open and said, "Go on in."

The sheriff was combing his hair as they walked into the room. "I see you survived the welcoming committee," Ted teased.

"I'll welcome their committee when I find out who did this," the sheriff responded with a smile. "Let's go home and get some sleep and we'll start all over again Monday after a restful weekend."

"Before we do," Larry said. "We've something that we would like to show you. You and Faith were still unconscious when we brought you in, and there was someone else we found after she was shot…"

"After we brought you two into the hospital in my truck," Larry finished explaining as they approached the woman's room, "They did emergency surgery on her which went fine."

"What connection do you think there may be?" Faith asked.

"I found out earlier that she wants to adopt the baby," Larry explained. "Why else would she be at the old house but to try to find the baby and risk her life for it?"

"That's a good point," the sheriff agreed. With a look of concern, he continued. "However, she should let our department handle this for her own safety."

"I agree and this is a good lead," Larry said. "Let's come back Monday morning and see what she can tell us about her being at the old house tonight. The doctor says she'll be well enough to talk then."

The sheriff left instructions with the doctor to contact his office if need be and guards were posted outside the woman's door for the different night shifts with instructions also to contact the sheriff if need be and then the sheriff and the others went home.

Death Notice

Saturday and Sunday passed without incident and all five detectives rested and took part in Sunday morning and evening church services with their families. Monday morning promised quiet as well. Life being the way it is though; it threw them a sharp curve.

Larry had just sat down to a lunch of turkey sandwiches and a soft drink when the phone rang.

"Hello?" Penny answered.

"Penny," came a familiar voice. It was the sheriff. "You and Larry round up the other three and go out to the old Bruntner place. When you get there, I'll explain why I had you to go out there."

"Okay, Daddy," Penny said and hung up the phone. She looked around at Larry. "Daddy wants us to go to the old house. He wants us to bring Ted and the girls with us."

"Perhaps we'll get to the bottom of this yet," he said and took a bite of his sandwich.

*****   *****   *****

Even in the bright August sunlight, the old house was forbidding. None of them like to be there, but there was no backing out now. The sheriff's car was already in the drive when the others arrived. Ted parked right behind it, and they all went into the old house and met Sheriff Rivers in the living room.

"What's up?" Larry asked.

"We don't know who," Sheriff Rivers began, "but someone tried to kill our friend at the hospital this morning."

"How?" Penny asked.

"She was lying in her bed when an uninvited visitor came into her room and shot her with a pistol that had a silencer on it. Not bothering to see if she was dead, he left, and a nurse saw him coming out of her room in a hurry. Seeing that the woman had been shot, she immediately reported it to the doctor on duty, and it was later reported to me. The woman is now doing fine," Sheriff Rivers explained.

"Is anything known about the man who pulled the trigger?" Ted asked.

"No," the sheriff replied. "The nurse said that it all happened too fast that all she saw was the back of the man. I have found out a few things about our friend, though," the sheriff continued to explain as he passed some papers around. "A hiker found an abandoned car this morning not far from the old house. We ran the Georgia plates that are on the car, and it's registered to a Norma Rockler. We were able to get a picture of her."

"And Norma Rockler is lying in the hospital with a couple of bullet wounds?" Larry guessed.

"Exactly," his dad agreed. He went on. "Even though the nurse did not see the assailant, a witness in the parking lot saw him get into an old brown pickup and come this way. And the driver was in a hurry. The witness said that the license plate was all bent out of shape and caked with mud."

"Has the truck been found out here?" Faith asked.

"No, not yet," Sheriff Rivers said. "But we are combing the countryside. I want to make a thorough search of this house, and we'll meet back in one hour."

"Let's, you and I, take the back of the house, Ted," Larry said.

"Faith and I will take the upstairs," Cherry volunteered and was gone before Faith could say yes or no.

"Let's, you and I, look around in the front of the house," the sheriff said to Penny and walked to the front door.

*****   *****   *****

"The others ought to be coming," Penny replied, looking at her watch. "I have 2:30 p.m."

"It has been an hour," the sheriff commented.

"It's also been a fruitless hour," came Faith's voice from the stairs. "Not a clue anywhere."

"Where's Larry and Ted?" Cherry asked.

In answer to her question, an arrow flew from out of nowhere and struck the wall a few feet from Penny's head. With lightning reflexes, Sheriff Rivers pulled Penny to the floor and the rest followed. They stayed down there a few minutes, but nothing else happened. Slowly, they all rose and looked at the deadly arrow. A note was tied to it which the sheriff removed. Having opened it, he read it aloud.

> With only an hour to go,
> Your friend will never know.
> And unless you act fast,
> He'll never last!

"They were in the back of the house!" Penny declared.

"We've got to get to them!" Faith put in as she led the way to where Larry and Ted went to search the house.

Eight

Deadly Explosion

After they had gone their separate ways through the house, Larry and Ted came upon an old room that had been the den at one time. An old desk was in the middle of the floor and toward the back wall. Larry carefully looked through the desk as Ted examined the wall shelves behind the desk. They sifted through cobwebs and dust that had been there for years.

Ted had found all kinds of books about the American Civil War and WWII. Ted found one book filled with pictures from Pearl Harbor to the treaty that was signed in Tokyo Bay. "Bruntner must have been a history buff about the Civil War and World War II. Find anything interesting?"

"Yes, I did," Larry replied. "Look at this."

He pulled a drawer out and Ted could only look wordlessly. Even though the desk was dusty, the drawer was clean and dust free, Larry pulled it all the way out and carefully looked the drawer over. On the back was a small piece of paper that had been caught in the corner. Larry carefully pulled the paper free and opened it. He read aloud these words: "Storage room at end of the hall."

"Let's check it out," Ted suggested.

They walked out into the hall. The hall went to the left toward an old stairway that led down to the basement. To the right, it continued for about thirty feet and made a right turn. They passed some bedroom doors as they went down the hallway and around the corner. The hall continued for about another fifteen feet and then made a dead-end stop. There were two doors, one on either side of the hallway. Larry and Ted went straight to the end of the hallway and examined the wall for any hidden doors just in case there might be any. Their search was in vain because it was an ordinary wall.

"Let's look in these two bedrooms," Ted replied. "We might find something of interest that will help."

"I'll take this room," Larry said as he entered the room on the right.

Larry shined his light around the room and saw that it had only a double bed and a nightstand. On the right side of the closet, Larry saw a door and walked over to it. He frowned as he stared at the door, wondering what was on the other side. A minute or two later, he turned to walk away when someone struck him from behind. He slumped to the floor unconscious. A few minutes later, Ted came into the room, and before he could call out to Larry, he, too, was struck from behind.

*****　　　*****　　　*****

It seemed like a dream, and it was in slow motion. Larry could hear ticking as it sounded like a clock. Among the ticking, he could hear a girl's voice calling him, but he tried to pay it no attention, but the voice was insistent on his coming with her. Suddenly, he felt strong hands grasp him and carry him away from the ticking clocks. He tried to argue but was suddenly jolted to life by a loud explosion. After the dust had settled, Larry looked around him and saw that he was in the backyard of the old mansion.

The remains of an old building were burning to the ground and smoke was climbing into the air. He saw that the sheriff was pouring water into the smoke and flame from a nearby creek. Larry tried to get up to help him, but he fell back down, holding his head.

"What hit me?" he questioned.

"From the size of that bump," Faith began. "I'd say a forty-pound sledgehammer."

"It felt more a forty-ton truck," Larry remarked, holding his head as he leaned back against a rock. Suddenly, and in pain, he sat up. "Where's Ted?" he questioned.

"That's what we were going to ask you," Cherry answered. She looked toward the smoldering building that Larry had been in. "He wasn't in there with you."

Larry studied the smoldering building for a few minutes and then looked back toward the old house. "The bedroom!" he called out.

Getting to his feet, he led the way back into the old house and up to the bedroom where he'd been struck down. Lying in the middle of the floor, they found Ted, still out.

Larry, Faith, and Cherry gathered around Ted as they worked to revive him. After a minute or so, Ted began to stir and slowly sat up. After a few seconds, he sat up completely, and then he stood to his feet.

"I believe I will make it," he said, holding his head as he leaned against the wall.

"Hey, everyone!" Penny called out from the direction of the closet. "Look what I found."

They gathered around Penny as her light revealed the door that had been locked was now opened. Larry and Penny flashed their lights down a dark hallway. At the end of the long hall, there was another door.

"Shall we?" Larry asked.

"Lead on," Ted replied.

Larry looked at his sister. "Tell Dad we're down here and that we're looking around."

As Penny went to get Sheriff Rivers, the rest walked down the hall that went to the door at the other end, not knowing what or who was behind it.

Nine

The Baby Reappears

Larry swung the door open on creaky hinges. As everyone trained their flashlights into the darkness beyond, they saw that it was a room filled with old dusty furniture.

The furniture consisted of chairs and tables that were buried in dust. After a few minutes of poking around, Penny came upon an old table with a piece of paper sticking out of a drawer. She pulled it out and looked it over. After a few minutes, she gave the paper to the sheriff.

He looked it over and looked back at Penny. Both had turned white. The sheriff turned the paper over, but the backside was blank. He went back to the front and reread what was there. After a few minutes, he said to the others, "Everyone listen to this."

They all gathered around the sheriff as he began to read, "Wanted, Norma Rockler. Height is five feet, five inches, blond hair, blue eyes. No aliases are known."

"That description could fit any number of women," Ted commented.

"Not when there is a picture with the poster," Sheriff Rivers said and gave the picture poster to Ted.

The poster passed from hand to hand as each one took a look at the girl in the picture. The picture was the same woman that was in the hospital. After a few minutes, Sheriff Rivers broke the silence.

"I'm going back to the office to check on this wanted poster," he explained. "There's something wrong, and I'm going to find out what it is. You five come with me because I have an errand that I need for you to do."

***** ***** *****

"I have a couple of men checking out the poster," the sheriff explained when they were back in his office. "It won't take very long by way of computer, and we should get word back at any time. In the meantime, I want you to check on Joe Chambers. We have not seen or heard anything of him since this whole thing began. Find out where he's been and what he's been up to."

"I would like to find out who put us in that wooden cage," Ted put in.

"You'll find out in time," the sheriff stated. "Meanwhile, see what you can find out about Joe Chambers. Go all over town and ask friends. Make it uncomfortable for him."

There came a knock at the door and a deputy entered. "There is no one listed in the wanted files that match the poster that was found at the house," he reported.

The deputy left and the sheriff looked at the others. "When you have been in law enforcement as long as I have, you tend to sense and know when something is not right in a case like this. I had a feeling all along that the poster was of no account. It was not put through the proper channels. Had it been put through the proper channels, I would have been notified by teletype and the computer. No such notifications were received here. This is another point against Chambers."

"Think that Chambers might have printed it?" Larry asked.

"Find Chambers and we'll find out for sure," the sheriff said.

***** ***** *****

Larry made his way to a mechanic's shop where a couple of his friends worked. He passed a picture of Chambers around, but none

26

of the mechanics recognized him. Larry then moved on to a small grocery store and again passed the picture around. Luck smiled on him this time. The store's owner did recognize the picture and a couple of customers did too. Larry got all the details, thanked them, and then moved on.

The other four, however, had no luck at all to get anyone to recognize their pictures. They had tried all the other stores in town and found no one who had seen, nor heard, anything of Chambers. After their searching, they all met back at the sheriff's office.

The clock on the wall in the sheriff's office showed the time to be 3:30 p.m. as Larry and the others come back to report their findings. "None of us had any luck," Penny began, looking at her brother. "Except Larry."

They looked at Larry as he began. "Yesterday afternoon, he went to guy's grocery and bought enough food to fill four sacks. A couple of customers remember him being there?"

"Did anyone remember seeing where he went?" Sheriff Rivers asked.

"Yes," Larry continued. "He was last seen going up Arrowhead Mountain on Interstate 67 toward Passville. A licensed number was obtained, and here it is."

The sheriff looked at the license number and said, "I'll pass this along and see if we can find our man."

"What would he be doing in Passville with four sacks of groceries?" Penny wondered.

"I don't know, Hon," the sheriff said with a frown. "But I do not like it." Silence filled the room until the phone rang breaking the silence. Sheriff Rivers answered it. Standing up, he replied, "We're on our way!" He looked at the others. "The baby that was put on our doorstep has turned up suddenly again at home!"

Ten

Larry Disappears

Everyone filed into the living room where Mrs. Rivers was with the baby.

"Who brought it here?" Sheriff Rivers asked.

"He was on the front porch when I heard it," Mrs. Rivers said. "I had been in the sewing room making Penny a blouse. I came in here to the living room to make a phone call and that is when I heard him crying on the front porch. The little thing was nearly throwing a fit, and I brought him in here. After I got him settled down, I called you."

"We are going to make sure that he doesn't slip away from us this time," the sheriff said, looking at the others around him. "I want this baby kept in sight at all times."

"Was there a note or anything else with the baby?" Larry asked walking to the window.

"Just this bottle," his mother answered. "I was careful not to get my prints on it when I picked it up. I knew that your father would want to dust it for prints."

"Indeed, I do," the sheriff replied.

He carefully wrapped the bottle in a clean cloth and gave it to Penny. "Take this to my office so it can be dusted for prints."

"Okay," Penny answered. She looked at Faith and Cherry. "Want to ride along?"

"Sure," they agreed.

"We'll be back for supper," Penny told her mother.

"Just be careful," Mrs. Rivers said as the girls walked out the front door. She shut the door and walked past the window that Larry was looking out.

"After a few minutes of deep thought, Sheriff Rivers noticed the intense look on Larry's face as he studied the field across the driveway. "What do you see, Son?"

"I have been through that field I don't know how many times," he explained. "But there is something different. And, for the life of me, I can't put my finger on it."

Larry continued to study the field as Mrs. Rivers came back into the living room and took the baby into the bedroom. After a few minutes, he turned to Ted and his dad. "I am more puzzled as to *who* put the baby on our front porch as to why."

"It does get one's curiosity," Ted agreed.

"That's it!" Larry suddenly exclaimed.

"What's it?" Sheriff Rivers asked.

"I know who left the baby on our porch," he replied. "But I need more time to get my facts together."

Before the sheriff or Ted could say another word, Larry was out the door and into his pickup.

"Where's he going?" Ted wondered as Larry drove away.

"On his way to solving this mystery," the sheriff answered.

Ted looked at Sheriff Rivers as though he had lost his mind. Smiling, the sheriff added, "Trust me."

***** ***** *****

"Where's Larry?" Mrs. Rivers asked, noting the time was 6:00 p.m.

"I wish I knew," the sheriff said with a worried tone. "He's been gone for over two hours."

Penny picked up the phone and dialed the Lightner's number. A couple of rings later, she said, "Hello, Faith? Larry wouldn't be over there would he?" After a few minutes, she continued. "He left a few minutes after we did, saying something about he knew who left the baby on our front porch. You have not seen him, though? Okay. Well, thanks. Bye."

Penny hung up stating, "He's not been over there."

The phone rang and Penny answered it. "Hello?"

A deep husky voice came over the phone. "Stay away from the old Bruntner place, or else you'll never see the light of day again!"

"Who is this?" Penny demanded.

"Your brother will never return. Too bad for him, because he'll burn!'"

There was a chuckle that sent shivers up and down Penny's spine, and then the phone went dead!

Eleven

A False Lead

Penny was stunned for a few seconds until her daddy's voice jolted her back to life. "Was that Larry?"

"N-no," she stammered, looking at him. "I don't know who that was. The caller gave a warning to stay away from the old Bruntner house and that..."

Her voice trailed off.

"And what?" the sheriff asked.

Penny looked at her daddy again. "And another message that said, 'Your brother will never return, too bad for him because he'll burn!'"

Silence filled the room for a few seconds until the ringing telephone shattered it. "Hello?" he answered. A few seconds later, he said, "We'll be right there!"

"You stay here with the baby. There'll be a deputy stationed outside at all times," the sheriff said as he went to the door. He looked at his daughter. "The old Bruntner place is on fire!"

Penny looked at her momma and then followed her daddy out to the patrol car.

*****　　　*****　　　*****

Sheriff Rivers stopped his car as close as possible to the burning building. He and Penny ran over to where the fire chief was standing.

"Hello, Sheriff, Miss Rivers," the chief greeted them.

"Jim," the sheriff began excitedly, "we received an anonymous phone call that this house was on fire and a warning that Larry was inside. Have you seen Larry at all?"

"I have not seen him, Sheriff," the chief explained, looking at the house. He continued slowly, "If he is in there, heaven help him."

They all looked at the house as a burning wall began to wobble and then collapse. After a few seconds, Penny buried her face into her dad's shoulder and sobbed uncontrollably.

Sometime after the sheriff arrived, Ted and his two sisters also arrived and joined with the sheriff and Penny going through the smoldering wood that was once an old, old house.

Nothing was said for a long time until Penny painfully replied, "I've found no clues, and I am afraid I will find what I do not want to see."

She again cried uncontrollably as Faith and Cherry took her back to the patrol car.

"There's something here that just doesn't seem quite right," the sheriff said. "Larry said he knew who had put the baby on our front porch and then he left."

"Mrs. Rivers called us after you left and explained to us what had happened," Ted explained. "According to the phone call, he should be up here, and he isn't, and we have not seen him."

"One of the things that bother me is that I do not see Larry's pickup," Sheriff Rivers explained, looking around him. "I'm going to start a search through these dense woods. It's got to be here, and there isn't much light left."

"Sheriff," Ted began. "Before you do, I have an observation I would like to point out."

"What is it?" the sheriff asked with interest.

"Larry never did say where he was going," Ted explained. "You came up here because of a phone call that said he was here. But, yet, we have not found him. And, as you said, his truck has not been found. It has occurred to me that someone has led us out here on a wild goose chase, as the saying goes."

The sheriff was thoughtful for a moment, and then he looked at Ted. "What would be the advantage of this?"

"I'm not sure," Ted went on. "But if my suspicions are correct, I would say that someone saw Larry leave the house and followed him. Whoever followed him may have found out Larry is on to them and feeling that Larry was putting them into a corner, led us here on this wild chase so…"

"So they could turn the tables on, Larry!" Sheriff finished.

"That's my observation," Ted replied.

"Sheriff!" Cherry called from the patrol car. "There is someone calling you on your two-way radio."

"Thanks," he called back as he walked over to the car. He picked up the microphone. "This is Sheriff Rivers."

"The Forestry Service reports an accident on Wide Creek, in the area of Narrow Curve," came a booming voice.

"Why are you telling me?" the sheriff asked. "Call the state patrol."

"This is the state patrol," the booming voice responded. Everyone looked at the radio as the voice continued. "The accident involves a pickup truck that is registered to Larry Rivers."

Twelve

Penny's Aces

"Is there any sign of Larry?" Penny asked anxiously as the pickup was being pulled up to the road from the shallow ravine.

"No sign yet, Miss Rivers," a forestry ranger replied. "We have searched the immediate area. As soon as more men arrive, we'll widen the search."

"Very well," the sheriff said. "Let us know if you find even a thread."

"Yes sir," the ranger replied and walked over to a group of his men.

The sheriff turned to one of his deputies. "I want Chambers brought in for questioning. Has he been found?"

"Yes, he has, Sheriff," came the answer. "The radio station was informed by the fire department about the fire and they told it over their last newscast. Chambers came storming into your office yelling about an arsonist setting the old house on fire. He is demanding swift action."

The sheriff frowned. "I can name the arsonist, and he will get his swift action sooner than he thinks. We are going back to the office and have a talk with him. Keep us informed of your progress, no matter which way it goes."

"Yes, sir," the deputy said.

*****   *****   *****

Things had not gone well for Chambers since he had come into the sheriff's office. A lighter had been found at the scene of the fire and it had the letters *JC* engraved on it. Fingerprinting analysis proved the prints on the lighter belonged to Joe Chambers.

Chambers' steel-blue eyes could not face Sheriff Rivers as he was being questioned.

"Where were you all day today?" the sheriff asked.

"In Passville," Chambers muttered.

"Can you prove it?"

"No," he muttered again.

"I didn't think so," Sheriff Rivers said. "That baby was put on our front doorstep with a bottle of milk and your prints were found all over it. And since you had not been seen around for a while, we circulated your picture around the country and in Passville. There's been quite a lot going on since you were last seen, and I believe you are right in the middle of it."

"You cannot prove it!" Chambers exclaimed.

"Oh, I believe that I can," Sheriff Rivers replied calmly, sitting back in his chair. He continued. "It occurs rather odd that a man would buy an old house and hardly be seen around it. The house was quiet until you bought it and then strange things began to happen. I don't much believe that I have to explain. If I were to buy an old house, I'd spend as much of my free time as possible fixing it up, unless I was up to no good."

"You have nothing on me!" Chambers shouted.

"Then, why are you yelling?" Ted asked.

Chambers slumped back in his chair, looking toward the floor.

"Penny has come up with some logical ideas that I believe you ought to hear," Sheriff Rivers said. He looked at his daughter. "Your witness."

"You were last seen going up Arrowhead Mountain," explained Penny. "Right before then, you were last seen with four sacks of groceries from here in town. You say you went to Passville, and I say that you were not there."

Chambers kept his stare toward the floor.

"I am calling your hand with four aces," Penny sternly went on. Ace number 1: As I said, you bought four sacks of groceries and went up Arrowhead Mountain. Why buy four sacks of groceries here when you can buy the same four over in Passville? Ace number 2: After all of this, the baby very mysteriously reappears with a bottle that has your fingerprints on it. Ace number 3: After looking through the living room window at the field across the driveway, Larry suddenly says he knew who put the baby on our steps and goes out the door. Ace number 4: Shortly thereafter, Larry disappears and is supposedly reported at the old Bruntner place which is also on fire. Then, a call comes through that his truck is in a ravine on Wide Creek. Evidence of a dented fender and chipped paint as well as disturbed gravel that leads to the ravine suggests to me that my brother had been forced off the road. The sheriff's lab is testing samples from Larry's truck and yours. If they match with what we already have, I'll do my best to see you're in jail for a long, long time."

Just as Penny finished, a woman came into the sheriff's office and said, "The paint samples match perfectly."

"You have cornered me!" Chambers wailed, standing to his feet. He grabbed a letter opener from the sheriff's desk and grabbed the woman and pointed it at her throat. Everyone sat motionless, not daring to move as he tighten his sinister grip on her.

Thirteen

On Laurel Creek

"Don't be a fool!" the sheriff tried to reason with Chambers. "You already have serious charges against you, do not add more charges of kidnapping."

"Just don't be a hero," Chambers ordered. "Everyone move over to the far corner."

They did as he said. Ted, however, tried to inch his way closer but Chambers tighten his grip on the woman and held the opener to her throat as he moved toward the door after everyone was in the far corner.

"Don't follow and she will be all right. Follow and it's dust she will bite!" he recited, going out the door.

After they were gone, the sheriff said, "Let's get him!"

"Sheriff," Ted spoke up. "Before you do anything, I was able to put a homing device on Chambers' truck. So, all we have to do is follow him by way of the signal."

"Excellent!" the sheriff beamed.

"I have the receiver here." Ted held up a box that was the size of a pocket calculator. He turned it on, and a needle was pointed in the *north* direction.

"He's going from east to north onto Laurel Creek Road," Ted explained.

"But, why not Wide Creek?" Faith asked. "That's where Larry's truck was found."

"It's also on the other side of town," Sheriff Rivers explained. "I believe that he is taking the long way into Passville by way of the Blue Ridge Parkway."

"The range on this isn't far," Ted explained. "We should go."

"I have my car outside," Cherry said, looking at Ted, Penny, and Faith. "We can follow at a distance."

As they all went out the door, the sheriff replied hanging up the phone, "I will be behind you in my patrol car. But first, I want to check on the hostage. Bystanders indicated she has been released outside."

***** ***** *****

Faith's watch showed the time as 9:00 p.m., and it was dark. Ted and the girls were a couple of miles behind Chambers. In a sharp curve three-quarters of the way up the mountain, Cherry parked the compact car to the side of the road, and the sheriff stopped behind her.

"What's up?" Sheriff Rivers asked as he walked to the car.

"They have gone down one of these two logging roads," Ted said, studying the receiver. "I can't tell which one because the battery has gone dead."

"We'll split up and go down each one," Sheriff Rivers directed. "I'll take this one that goes down toward Bear Lake. Ted, you take the one on the left that goes toward and along Squirrel Ridge. If either one of us finds anything, we'll call the other one on the walkie-talkies. You girls stay here and monitor us on the county radio in my patrol car. Use it if you find or see anything unusual back this way."

"We'll be listening," Penny said.

Sheriff Rivers walked down the Bear Creek Trail, and Ted walked around the bend in the road and went down the other trail along Squirrel Ridge.

***** ***** *****

Ted had been walking for about fifteen minutes when his walkie-talkie crackled into life. Ted held it close to listen.

"Ted," came the sheriff's voice, "I have found an old truck and the engine is still warm. I am about…" The sheriff was suddenly cut off.

"Sheriff Rivers?" Ted questioned into the radio. Receiving no answer, Ted tried again. Finally, he called the girls.

"Ted," Penny called into her microphone, "I heard you trying to get Daddy."

She was fighting back tears as Ted's voice was heard. "You girls call in for backup. I am on my way back."

Ted was running before he had finished his sentence.

Fourteen

Rescued

"I called in for help," Penny explained as Ted walked up to the car.

"Good," he said. "I'm going back there and see what is going on. When help does arrive, send them in. And please keep the radio turned on."

The girls looked at Ted as Faith replied, "Just be careful."

"I'll call in every five minutes," Ted assured her.

"We'll be listening," Cherry said.

Ted walked down the old logging road that Sheriff Rivers had walked down less than thirty minutes before. He walked, shining his light only when he had to. Even though the tree leaves were thick in cover overhead, the moon was shining brightly onto the road. Every once in a while, he'd come to a darken area and he would use his flashlight. And as promised, he called in every five minutes. Ted had been walking for about ten minutes when he heard Cherry's voice over the radio. "Ted, there are two county patrol trucks here."

"Have them come on back," Ted instructed. "I have found the old brown truck Sheriff Rivers was talking about, and I see no one else is around."

"We're coming," Cherry informed him.

"I will look around here and see what I can find until you get here," Ted replied.

He looked the truck over and could not find anything at all. After another few minutes, he heard a vehicle coming from further up the road that he had not been to explore. He hid on a small ridge below the road behind a tree and watched silently as another pickup roared past him and on toward the others that were coming. Ted raised the radio antenna as he watched the truck. "Faith," he began. "There is company coming in an old rusted colored pickup. He is going fast, so be watching for him."

"Deputy Young says he is going to make a roadblock with his truck," Faith answered.

"I am coming back at a run," Ted concluded. He climbed back on the road and ran at full speed.

***** ***** *****

Unknowingly, though, the rust-colored truck was coming toward the roadblock. The fleeing truck rounded a curve and skidded to a halt. A man jumped out and fired a pistol, sending everyone for cover. He then pulled two captives from the cab. Chambers waved a gun at them as he yelled, "I've got your sheriff and his nosey son. I will drop them both if you don't move the roadblock!"

"All right," the deputy answered. He climbed back into his truck and the rest did too. The deputy had to back up until he came to a wide spot where he could turn around. He then slowly proceeded toward the forest service road with Chambers following.

Penny was tearful and made no effort to hide her emotions. Faith comforted her as best as possible. After a few minutes, the deputy called out, "He stopped."

***** ***** *****

The truck had been following the others when the back left tire went flat. Chambers stopped the truck and started to the tire when a flying fist came from out of nowhere and sent him to the ground. His assailant had him pinned to the ground before he could regain his wits. Footsteps came running up as Faith and Cherry remained at the front of Chambers' truck.

"You all right, Ted?" Faith called out.

"Yeah, I'm fine," he answered. He looked at the deputy. "Cuff him, please."

Once he was cuffed, Ted walked over to the passenger door and helped the sheriff and Larry out. Ted untied Sheriff Rivers as Penny untied Larry. There followed a tearful reunion, and in a few minutes, Larry looked at Penny.

"We got him, sis," he said with a smile.

"We'll have his friends by morning as well," the sheriff added.

Penny looked at her brother. "How did you ever manage to get yourself kidnapped by Chambers?"

"There's plenty of time for questions and answers tomorrow," Larry replied. "But for tonight, it's a good night's sleep for me. I have had quite a day of it, and I'm bushed."

Standing between his two sisters, Ted smiled and suggested, "Let's go to the house."

They loaded up and started down the mountain road, feeling satisfied that they had accomplished a happy ending.

Fifteen

Surprising Answers

The day dawned bright and beautiful. It was now three days later, and everyone gathered into the Rivers' living room. Along with the sheriff and his family and the Lightners were Norma Rockler, her husband, and the baby. The sheriff stood before the fireplace and called for everyone's attention.

"There are few things that have to be cleared up," the sheriff began. "So we'll start at the beginning."

"To begin with," Mrs. Rivers said, looking from the baby to her husband. "Who kidnapped the baby?"

"Two of Chambers' men," Sheriff Rivers answered, walking over toward the Rockler's.

"For some twisted reason," Mr. Rockler began. "He just had to have me help him or he would do great harm to the baby and my wife. We were, and still are very much interested in adopting this baby, and I agreed to help him. All I did was stay in the house to scare off anyone who came in that wasn't supposed to be there. He kept the baby in a well-equipped nursery. This nursery was not in the old house. He used another small, abandoned house that had been closed up for some time. When I had my chance, I brought the baby back here, and then I was going back to bring Chambers into you. But I did not know that I was being followed by Chambers. He also shot the arrow into your door to get you out of the kitchen so he could get the baby again. This baby was his assurance that I would help. Even

43

though he threatened me with bodily harm if I tried again, I never gave up looking for a way to bring the baby back here. I was later able to bring the baby back here to your house. This time, I watched to make sure that the baby was found. When it was, I went to the hospital and stayed with my wife until she was able to come home."

"What did the notes mean?" Mrs. Rivers asked.

"There were portraits Bruntner had there at one time of his various family members," Larry began. "When Chambers was in prison before, his cellmate was telling him about the portraits believing that they were very valuable works of art. The cellmate had heard Bruntner telling about them when he was in a restaurant sitting at the next table from Mr. Bruntner. The cellmate had gotten only a few words about the portraits and somehow believed that they were very valuable. The last line of the first note," Larry explained, "Chambers believed that if he could get hold of these portraits, he could sell them and be financially set for life, thinking that it would be a sweet life for him. What he didn't know and would learn later after we caught him is that these portraits were of family members and not valuable like he thought they were. The second note is somewhat self-explanatory if you stop and think about the word *rattle*. All along, I'd guessed what Chambers finally told in the end: rattlesnakes. Chambers was going to spring them on us. Fortunately, he never got the chance."

"I'm sorry I asked," Mrs. Rivers shivered.

"It was me who called you that night," Mrs. Rockler put in. "We were first led to the baby orphanage in White Pine by my sister who lives there. I remember seeing Chambers there for the first time in White Pine the day before all this started. That is when he noticed my husband and the next thing we know, the baby was gone. I had been following the man who had been following my husband and after he had taken the baby, I followed him out the road until he stopped. I tried to get the baby back, but he fled away. I continued to follow him to get the baby back. He came to the outskirts of Arrowhead County, parked his car and fled into the brush with the baby and I never did find them. I then found a phone and called you. Then before I could say anything, the kidnapper jerked the phone away and knocked me out cold. Later, I learned that while I was searching, he brought the baby back to the old house and my husband then was able to bring the baby here and put him on your back doorstep. The same man that I had been following thought that I had gotten the baby and came back looking for me."

"Where did Chambers get the money to buy the house if he had been in prison until recently?" Mr. Lightner questioned.

"The money he used was from a robbery some ten years ago," the sheriff answered. "He had hidden it before he was caught the first time. It has been found and recovered."

"When I first went to the mansion and Mr. Rockler met me at the door, I didn't know what to expect until he explained to me about wanting to adopt the baby and land Chambers and his men in jail. So we decided to play the game as it happened to really nail Chambers with some hard evidence," Larry explained.

"It was also Chambers' men that locked Cherry and me in that wooden dungeon," Ted put in. "After we came around, I noticed that it was all made of wood, or so I thought. I knew there had to be a way out of there. It was not until Cherry relit my lighter that I knew what had been nagging at me. The light was being reflected from the ceiling and that told me that was our way out. A large mirror had been put over the top as a roof. It was a two-way mirror so they could look down at us without our knowing it. After I helped Cherry out and I got out, I heard two men coming, so I hid. I learned later they were Chambers' men. They ran down the trail thinking that we had left the grounds and we have not seen them since."

"It was Chambers who forced us off the road." Penny took it from there. "He had us all under surveillance and knew our every move. He didn't want us to discover his true intentions and he tried to discourage us."

Penny walked over to Mrs. Rockler as she continued. "It was Chambers who shot you that night shortly after I got there to the mansion. He followed me there and you as well."

"I was on my way there to talk to you about seeking your help," Mrs. Rockler explained. "I called the sheriff's office, and they said you were on your way there."

"At the hospital," Larry looked at Mrs. Rockler. "I said I knew you wanted to adopt the baby because Mr. Rockler told me so at the mansion when we first met there."

"But who was it that shot Mrs. Rockler in the hospital," Mrs. Rivers asked.

"One of Chambers' men," her husband answered. "He acted on his own, thinking that with Beverly out of the way, they'd have only to contend with me. It was also a threat to me that the same would happen to me if I didn't cooperate."

Looking at the sheriff, Mrs. Rockler asked, "Wasn't there a deputy outside my room?"

"Yes," the sheriff replied, "he had heard a noise down the hall and went to investigate and was hit from behind and fell to the floor. It was the same guy that shot Mrs. Rockler."

"It was Chambers who shot that arrow in the old house to warn us away," Sheriff Rivers continued. "I was not about to give up and leave my son to die at the hands of a madman. It was Penny who found Larry, and I pulled him out just before the shed exploded."

"That was close," Larry said, still standing in front of the fireplace. "The desk drawer was clean because Chambers put that note in it to get us down to the storage room to find that wanted poster on Mrs. Rockler. The door was still locked when Ted and I got there. Chambers hadn't put the wanted poster on the table yet in the concealed room. He knocked Ted and me out and then put the poster on the table. After that, he put me outside in the old shed as Dad explained. That's why the door was locked when we got there and unlocked when Penny found it. He tried to frame Mrs. Rockler to get her out of the way. They were all bound and determined to get her out of the way."

"But where did he get the poster?" Mrs. Rockler asked.

"There was an old printing press in the attic that Mr. Bruntner used in his advertising business many years ago," the sheriff explained. "When Chambers found it, he got the idea to make the poster. He got your picture out of the White Pine News from the community section that said you were visiting your sister."

"What I don't understand," Penny said, looking at her brother. "Is that how you knew who put the baby on our front doorstep?"

"I knew that while Chambers had the baby, he also had his assurance that no one would really try to stop him," Larry explained. "When I was looking out the window, I could see what at the time I thought was moving bushes. Then I noticed that there was no wind. What I saw was one of Chambers' men hiding behind the bushes behind the driveway. What took me a few minutes to realize was that he was wearing camouflage. Then he moved across a gap in the bushes, and I realized that Mr. Rockler was being followed. As I said, knowing the baby was insurance to Chambers, I figured that Mr. Rockler put the baby on our front doorstep. I also believed that since he had a spy, this reinforced my thinking that it was Mr. Rockler who put the baby on the doorstep.

"Mr. Rockler waited around in hiding to see that the baby would be found. When Dad drove up, Mr. Rockler went to the hospital. The spy was skeptical about leaving at first but then decided to try. That is when I spotted him."

"I made sure that Chambers' fingerprints were on the bottle for more incriminating evidence," Mr. Rockler put in.

"It was Chambers who called about staying away from the old mansion and that Larry would burn," Penny explained, affectionately looking at her brother. He called the night Larry disappeared. Where did you go?"

"I was on my way to talk to Mr. Rockler about finding more evidence to put Chambers away," Larry answered. "I could not find Mr. Rockler at the old house, and I didn't think at the time that he'd gone to the hospital. So, I was on my way back home. As I went into Narrow Curve, Chambers suddenly came from the other direction and forced me off the road. As I went into the ravine, I hit my head on the steering wheel and the next thing I remember, I'm tied up in an old shack with Chambers glaring down at me."

"Chambers was on his way back to meet with his two men at the mansion," Ted explained further. "He and Larry coincidently met in the curve and Chambers forced him off the road. He had already set the house on fire and had been looking for Mr. Rockler, not knowing that he was at the hospital with his wife. As the house was burning, Chambers saw his chance to try to put a scare into us by calling here and saying that Larry was in the old house. He originally set the house on fire because he no longer wanted it, and he didn't want no one else to have it."

"Explain this to me, please." Faith spoke up. "Why did Chambers go down that old logging road?"

"There's an old cabin that belongs to some hunters about two miles down the old road," Sheriff Rivers explained. "One of Chambers men grew up over on Straight Creek, about five miles from here. He knew the cabin was there and Chambers used it. After Chambers had tied up Larry, he took him to the cabin and made us think that Larry was at the old house. Chambers' original plan was to do in Mr. Rockler. Then he was going to meet his men at the old house and then take out for South Carolina. Since they had Larry, the plan was changed to have Chambers come into my office and claim that an arsonist had caused the fire and he was going press charges. Only it didn't work out as he had planned."

"How did the tire go flat?" Cherry asked.

"When Chambers stopped and threatened the sheriff and Larry," Ted explained. "I jumped on the back of the truck. Before I did, I managed to wedge a nail that was in the back of his truck into the tread of the tire. As we rolled along, the nail worked its way into the tire, and it went flat. Y'all know the story from there."

"Not quite," Mr. Rockler said, looking at Mr. Lightner. "You stated that Chambers gave three times the asking price for the old mansion."

"Yes, I did," Mr. Lightner said.

Mr. Rockler looked at Larry. "You said the money came from a robbery about ten years ago."

"That's right," Larry agreed.

"I was wondering," Mr. Rockler continued. "Will Mr. Bruntner have to give it back?"

"I'm afraid so," Mr. Lightner answered. "He's wanting the land back for personal reasons. After all this, he's going to clear away the remains of the old house and rebuild it and remodel the other buildings. He's also going to rebuild that wooden dungeon Ted and Cherry were in."

"That wraps it up, then," Larry said.

"Not quite," his dad replied, walking toward the coffee table. "The county commissioners were really impressed with your performance that they've made you special detectives with the sheriff's department. Gather in front of the fireplace please."

With astonished looks, they gathered as requested. One by one, to Larry, Ted, Penny, Faith, and Cherry, the sheriff gave them special law enforcement badges. They were of silver content, and the cases were genuine leather. On the outside of each case was the name given to them by the county commissioners. A name they were proud to hold: The Arrowhead Mystery Detectives.

The sheriff read from a sheet of paper, "We, the commissioners of Arrowhead County, in the State of North Carolina, are proud to honor Larry Rivers, Ted Lightner, Penny Rivers, Faith Lightner, and Cherry Lightner as the best mystery detective team anyone could ever know and are also proud to have them join the sheriff's department. We know they will always live up to their team's name as they work to make our country, state, and county a better place to live and work in. May the protecting hand of the Lord be with you always in your endeavors to keep the people safe from harm."

"Thank you," Larry replied. "Even though this is totally unexpected, we will always do the best that we can, and we know that He will always lead us. It's our constant prayer that the Lord will be our guide as we take on this new responsibility."

And with that, everyone gave them a standing ovation, and these five knew that they could *never* let their people down. They vowed to do the job that was before and appointed unto them, even at the point of death.

They would truly need His help and guidance when they encountered their next case, *The Mystery of the Vanishing Detectives.*

The end of book one.

(For he saith, I have heard thee in a time accepted,
and in the day of salvation have I succored thee: behold,
now is the accepted time; behold, now is the day of salvation.)

—2 Corinthians 6:2 (KJV)

The Plan of Salvation

Perhaps you have been asked many questions that are of vital importance to you. Here's another one: where will you spend all of eternity?

Jesus gave his life on the cross for all of us that we can be with Him in eternity. However, in order to be with Him, the sinner must accept Him. The sinner must confess or acknowledge their sins. We are told in 1 John 1:9, "If we confess our sins, he is faithful and just to forgive us our sins, and to cleanse us from all unrighteousness."

John 3:7 tells us, "Ye must be born again." You must be saved by putting your faith and trust in Him when you ask Him to save you from your sins.

There are those that might say they have never sinned. They are wrong. "For all have sinned and come short of the glory of God" (Romans 3:23).

You see, "for the wages (or payment) of sin is death" (Romans 6:23). This is the separation from God, and the sinner will spend all eternity in that awful place the Bible calls hell.

The scripture I quoted in the Car Payment (*Along Life's Way, Volume 1*, pages 83–84) is used here: "And as it is appointed unto men once to die, but after this, the judgment." All of us are going to be judged. Will He judge you as a sinner or one of His children?

There is good news, there is hope.

He loved us that much that He bore all our sins on Calvary's cross. He suffered, bled, and died in our place so that we would not have to spend eternity in hell. "For God so loved the world, that he gave his only begotten Son, that whosoever believeth in him should not perish, but have everlasting life" (John 3:16).

Second Corinthians 5:21 tells us that He was made to be sin for us "*that we might be the righteousness of God in Him.*"

"*For the life of the flesh is in the blood*" (Leviticus 17:11). "*Without shedding of blood is no remission* (or pardon)" (Hebrews 9:22). Romans 5:8 tells us that "*God commanded His love toward us, in that while we were yet sinners, Christ died for us.*

I ask that you confess your sins now to Him and ask that He save you and cleanse you from all unrighteousness and that He will guide you daily as the Comforter takes His abode (John 14:16).

Romans 10:13 tells us "For whosoever shall call upon the name of the Lord shall be saved."

Call upon Him now before it's too late. Second Corinthians 6:2 tells us that today is the accepted time of salvation. Not tomorrow (Proverbs 27:1), not next week, or next month. *Today* is the accepted time to accept Him and His free gift of salvation.

Please don't wait. Accept Him now in your heart and life as you journey along life's way.

We will do our best to pray for you that you will accept Him.

Remember, what you determine to do with the Lord Jesus Christ today determines where you'll spend eternity.

About the Author

Jack White has always loved telling stories and listening to the stories that other people are telling. He has enjoyed writing and collecting these stories over the years. He now hopes that these stories will be a blessing to his readers. For the detective stories, each book is its own story. He wants the readers to know that there is a plan of salvation (at the end of the book).

He was born in Canton, Ohio, but grew up just outside Dellroy, Ohio. He joined the US Army two months out of high school, served three years, was honorably discharged. He would be in the reserves for about four to five years. To include his reserve time, he has just over a ten-year break in active service but was accepted back on active duty in 1986 and finished out his time for retirement. And as of December 31, 2001, he retired as a sergeant after serving for twenty years and is also a disabled veteran. He now lives in Asheboro, North Carolina, with his wife, Ann, of forty-eight years. He also loves to visit historic places. They have two children—a daughter, Penny (Clint) Pratt of Asheboro, North Carolina, and a son, Larry White, in Asheboro, North Carolina, Illinois. He is retired from the Illinois Secretary of State. He loves being with his family and traveling in his free time. He also enjoys Christian music and loves going to church as often as he can.